Rookie reader®

Messy Bessey's HOLIDAYS

by
Patricia
and
Fredrick
McKissack

illustrated by Dana Regan

DATE DUE

DATE DUE		
AUG 1 4 2010		

Children's Press ®
A Division of Grolier Publishing
New York • London • Hong Kong • Sydney
Danbury, Connecticut

To Roberta and Phil Duyff–thanks for the many holiday celebrations.
—P. and F. M.

To the Regans
—D. R.

Reading Consultant
Linda Cornwell
Learning Resource Consultant
Indiana Department of Education

Visit Children's Press® on the Internet at:
http://publishing.grolier.com

Library of Congress Cataloging-in-Publication Data
McKissack, Pat.
   Messy Bessey's holidays / by Patricia and Fredrick McKissack; illustrated by
Dana Regan.
      p. cm. — (Rookie reader)
   Summary: Bessey and her mother bake cookies for Christmas, Kwanzaa, and
Hanukkah, and after cleaning up the kitchen, they distribute the treats to their
neighbors.
   ISBN 0-516-20829-2 (lib. bdg.)   0-516-26476-1 (pbk.)
   [1. Baking—Fiction. 2. Cleanliness—Fiction. 3. Christmas—Fiction.
4. Kwanzaa—Fiction. 5. Hanukkah—Fiction. 6. Stories in rhyme.]
I. McKissack, Fredrick. II. Regan, Dana, ill. III. Title. IV. Series.
PZ8.3.M224Mds 1999
[E]—dc21   98-8057
                                CIP
                                AC

Recipe on page 31 adapted from Betty Crocker's New Cookbook, *1996. Used with
permission of General Mills, Inc.*

GROLIER
PUBLISHING

December holidays are great—
a time for fun and cheer.

Christmas, Kwanzaa, Chanukah and the coming New Year.

Bessey's in the kitchen
busy as can be
baking holiday cookies
for her friends and family.

Ummm!
Those cookies smell so good.
They're sure to taste good, too.

8

But Messy Bessey look around.
There is something you must do.

While working
you have made a mess.
Things are out of place.

Keep your kitchen safe and clean
by wiping up your space.

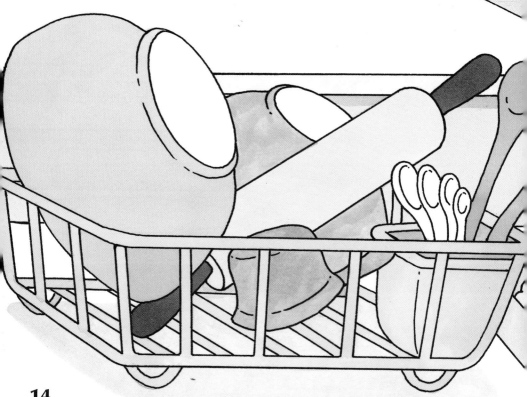

Wonderful job, Miss Bessey!
The kitchen looks just great.

Your cookies tell a story
of how we celebrate.

Eight menorah candles
lit each and every night
of the Jewish Chanukah holiday,
a festival of light.

20

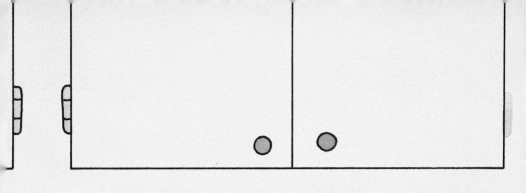

These are happy angels
who sang on Christmas morn
to shepherds on a hillside
that Jesus Christ was born.

KWANZAA

unity

self-determination

collective work and
responsibility

cooperative economics

purpose

creativity

faith

African-Americans' Kwanzaa
is a week of community sharing.
Families gather to feast and learn
through the seven ways of caring.

Menorahs, candles, fruits, and bells
are signs of the holidays.

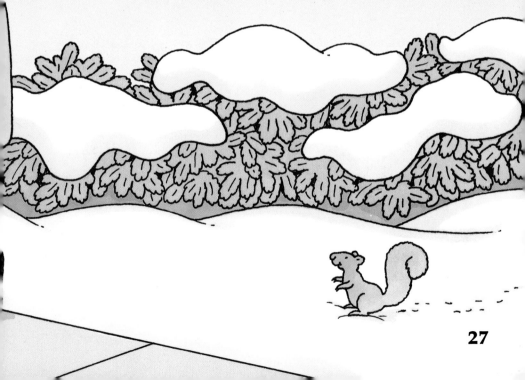

All over, people celebrate

in many different ways.

Christmas,
Kwanzaa,
and Chanukah,
no matter what the reason,
here's a gift from Bess to you
to celebrate the season.

DECORATED SUGAR COOKIES

*Ask an adult to help you make
these delicious holiday treats!*

*1 1/2 cups powdered sugar
1 cup margarine or butter, softened
1 tsp. vanilla
1/2 tsp. almond extract
1 large egg
2 1/2 cups all-purpose flour
1 tsp. baking soda
1 tsp. cream of tartar*

1. Mix powdered sugar, margarine, vanilla, almond extract, and egg in large bowl. Stir in remaining ingredients. Cover and refrigerate at least 2 hours.

2. Heat oven to 375°. Grease cookie sheet lightly with shortening.

3. Divide dough in half. Roll each half 1/4-inch thick on lightly floured surface. Cut into desired shapes with 2- to 2 1/2-inch cookie cutters. Place on cookie sheet.

4. Bake 7 to 8 minutes or until edges are light brown. Remove from cookie sheet. Cool on wire rack.

5. Frost and decorate cooled cookies with frosting, tinted with food coloring. Decorate with colored sugar, small candies, fruit, or nuts if desired.

Makes about 5 dozen 2-inch cookies.

Word List

(132 words)

a
African-Americans
all
and
angels
are
around
as
baking
be
bells
Bess
Bessey
Bessey's
born
busy
but
by
can
candles
caring
celebrate
Chanukah
cheer
Christ
Christmas
clean
coming
community
cookies
December

different
do
each
eight
every
families
family
feast
festival
for
friends
from
fruits
fun
gather
gift
good
great
happy
have
her
here's
hillside
holiday
holidays
how
in
is
Jesus
Jewish
job
just
keep
kitchen

Kwanzaa
learn
light
lit
look
looks
made
many
matter
menorah
menorahs
mess
messy
Miss
morn
must
new
night
no
of
on
out
over
people
place
reason
safe
sang
season
seven
sharing
shepherds
signs
smell

so
something
space
story
sure
taste
tell
that
the
there
these
they're
Things
those
through
time
to
too
ummm
up
was
ways
we
week
what
while
who
wiping
wonderful
working
year
you
your